R~ Words
The seX Files
Encounters 1-8
By Maricca Fox Darling
Copyright © 2014

Table of Contents:

Dedication

This book is dedicated to those in committed relationships and married couples. Commitments can win with the right tools. Imagination is a powerful thing… use yours.

Note from the Author

For those who enjoy great erotica, but prefer less than hundreds of pages, R- Words are just for you. There is nothing like adding a spark to your bliss. Use your imagination and picture your spouse as the stranger at the bar, the person you met at a club, or someone you bumped into you at a bookstore. Tie their face to every fantasy you have as you enter a world designed to turn you on. I use a variety of triggers when it comes to anatomy, therefore I follow one rule, and that is to turn you on. So dim the lights, relax, and open your legs. You are about to experience R- Words, The seX Files.

Intro-Teaser

```
Pink Dynamite!
```

Similar to a volcano at its hottest peak, cum shot across the room like a super soaker. He looked at me as if shocked by the gravity of juices flowing from my body so I grabbed his hand and stuck two of his fingers inside me. Like a sensual animal, he rolled his body in rhythm with his winding fingers and cupped my pussy yet again. The sloshing sound of cum pressed against his palm as he smacked his hand in and out of my juicy flower filled the room. Moans rose from my belly and exited my voice box as he stuck his tongue in my mouth. Haaaa-haaaa-haaaaaaaaaaaaaaaaaaaaaaaaaaaaaaaaaaaaaaaaaaaaaaaaaa! Again, I squirted a massive amount of cum all over him, the sheets, and the wall. But this time he stuck his cock in my pussy while I was still releasing. My body jerked from head to toe, dancing against his in the most awkward motion. Although he didn't seem to mind, his facial expression was still that of someone who'd just witnessed something they couldn't explain. He began to pound his entire body down on top of mine over and over until he mimicked the previous movement of his fingers. I'll be damned if he didn't get it. Oh shit- oh shit- oh shit- oh shit- oh shit… SHIT! My toes curled and my thighs stiffened as my pussy erupted, smothering his dick with the juiciest penetration I'd ever had. He's the first man that ever made me squirt.

Pussy Power!

I must be crazy… I know like hell normal people can function in everyday life without hiding a constant hard on. Damn! So many women and just one dick. I can't fuck them all, but if I could just find one satisfying pussy to beat the hell out of on a regular basis, maybe, just maybe this shit could go down for a while.

"Next," she said, with low eyes and a cocked head. Although I sensed the attitude in her voice, I couldn't stop staring at her juicy lips. I stepped up to the counter and slid my deposit to the tips of her manicured fingers. Her nails were painted neutral, but clipped down very low, and she had short natural hair. I had a theory about chocolate girls but that shit was shot to hell three experiences ago. I guess I don't know women as well as I thought. Anyway, I swore I'd never fuck with a dark skinned girl again, and here I am… dick hard at the counter at the damn bank. Every time I see this chick I wonder…

"*Hellooo*," she sarcastically chanted, wiggling her fingers. "Can I get the cash to go with this slip please?"

"Oh yeah, sorry about that." I passed her the cash and watched her purse her lips as she counted the money. Her rude ass threw her purse on her shoulder before giving me my receipt. What kind of chick clocks out on the spot like that? Where is her boss anyway?

I turned around to leave but when her fine ass stepped from behind that counter my dick stood straight up. "Damn!" Before I knew it the word flew out of my mouth like an untrained child acting out in public. I know she looked back but my eyes were glued to her ass. Fitted cream slacks with no panty line, she had to have on a thong. Her waist was tight and she had small breasts but her body was so well-proportioned that all I could think about was watching her walk around in those thongs doing everything. Washing dishes, cooking, out to dinner, riding a bike, hell it didn't matter. She was a subtle version of fine as hell. I pulled out my cell phone and tried to pretend like I missed a call to divert any inappropriate attention I paid to her ass, but as I passed her, the alluring smell of her perfume mixed with her body chemistry slowed my steps. Dick still hard!

"Excuse me," she said, "do you always carry that thing around or is this a special occasion?"

"I'm sorry, are you talking to me?"

"No, I'm talking to your friend down there... You walk up to my counter all hard and shit, you staring at my ass like you've been in jail or something, and now you're lingering next to my car."

I know like hell I didn't follow this chick to her car. "I'm sorry Miss. I didn't mean to offend you, and I surely didn't mean to follow you."

"Okay," she said, standing there with her arms crossed. "So you gonna ask for my number or what?"

She can't be serious. This girl has no idea how bad I want to fuck her right now. "Why don't you put your number in my phone, Sweetheart?" I needed to make sure I had access to her.

My eyes roamed her body from head to toe as she typed her name and number in my phone. Amber. Attitude and all, I was digging her. With a weak wrist, she aimed the phone at me, "Don't wait two days to call, I don't have time for games," she said, right before walking around me to get in her car. I didn't know if it was her confidence that turned me on, or the fact that I knew I was going to fuck her. I watched Amber drive away as this thick red chick walked passed me. Something was off, I knew her ass was fat but I didn't bother to look back…

Later that night I must have checked my phone twenty times as if waiting for Amber to call or text me. It didn't dawn on me until the next morning when I woke up with blue balls that she didn't have my number. It's too early to call, I thought, but then again, she should be up getting ready for work… bump that, I'm calling. Voice mail? I knew I shouldn't have called. Man, I need to chill. *'Amber, it's Rico, we met at the bank the other day. Give me a call when you get this message.'*

Three days, two calls and four text messages later, and I still hadn't heard from her. What kind of game was *she* playing? And why did I put so much energy into this chick, I could have had ten chicks by now, shit ain't nobody got time for this. I talked shit alright, but I took my ass back to the bank. I waited by her car for her to get off work. As soon as she stepped out that door at 5:01 like I knew she would, my man stood at attention. Friday must be jean day, and she wore the hell out of those jeans. For a slim chick, she was kind of thick, I could see the shape of her ass from the front, and whoever came up with high heels and jeans together can have everything I own. She cut her eyes across the parking lot and walked to her car like a tall, sexy cat.

"So is this a wrong number you gave me? Is Amber your real name?"

She stood less than a foot away from me. So close that I could see all of the flaws on her face, but they too were sexy. I love a woman with no makeup.

"What did I tell you about walking around with your shit all hard?" she said.

"Time out- did you get my calls, my messages?"

"Yeah, I've been busy."

"Look, you told me not to play games and you sitting up here ignoring my outreach. I don't appreciate that."

She hit the alarm on her car and looked me in the eyes. "Listen, I have a life… and sometimes I get busy, so during those times I may not be at your disposal. And let's get something straight, you don't know me well enough to be checking me. Secondly, we both know what this is, so when I need you, I will return your call." She opened her car door. "Luckily for you I'm free tonight so if you want to do something let me know."

'Who the fuck does she think she is? She ain't all that! And *I'm* the mother fucking man. I make the demands.' "Alright, what would you like to do tonight?" I was weak for her and didn't know why.

"All types of shit." She leaned toward me and placed her thigh between my legs, damn! "But you can feed me first," she said.

I took her to one of the nicest restaurants in Atlanta, spent too much damn money for someone I may never see again, and I just knew she was gonna make up some story to end the night… but she didn't. She invited me back to her apartment. I drove through the gated community behind her and parked a few spaces back to avoid looking desperate. She got out of her car and waved me over while unlocking her door to her apartment.

"Give me a second," I yelled out the window.

She left the door cracked and went inside. I did everything I could including thinking about unattractive chicks to get my dick to go down before walking in. But that shit was pointless when I saw her standing in the kitchen pouring a glass of wine wearing peach boy shorts and a too little t-shirt. My shit pressed against my zipper until it became painful.

"You just don't listen, do you?" She handed me a glass of wine and unbuckled my belt. My heart beat pounded so hard, I know she heard it.

"Taste it and tell me what you think," she said, proceeding to unzip my pants.

I sipped the wine but I couldn't taste a damn thing. My senses were all focused on her. She dropped my jeans to the floor, and seductively slid my briefs down. I tossed the rest of the wine down in one shot and grabbed the back of her head, forcing her up to kiss me. Her lips melted into my mouth, softer than I thought they could ever feel. We could have kissed all night. She grabbed my dick with one hand and began stroking me. I wanted to fuck her so bad I could barely breathe. She pulled away from the kiss and looked up at me with wide innocent eyes as she lowered herself to the floor. With both hands she palmed my dick and winded her wrists in opposite directions while kissing the head. Next thing I knew, she was sucking the shit out of me. I bit my bottom lip in an effort not to scream, but suddenly she stopped. I looked at her, my chest heaving up and down.

"Take off your shorts," I said.

She laid on the floor and slid her boy shorts halfway down. I pulled them over her feet and spread her legs as I admired that sexy chocolate pussy. She had no smell at all down there, other than the aroma of light juices that I couldn't wait to taste. I took my thumbs and opened the lips to her pink circle. My hard dick pressed against the floor as I lay between her flower. Her body squirmed beneath me as she moaned and just like that, the power between us shifted. I was now in control of this confident, outspoken, sexy woman. Her entire body was begging for me, and I held nothing back. My tongue went so far up her pussy that her thighs trembled as her toes curled. She served me up with grinding motions as I forced her ass back down to the floor with my face. Her short nails caressed the back of my head, and even though she tasted ten times better than the expensive meal we shared, I wanted her to cum on my dick. Using my feet, I kicked my jeans off while still eating her pussy. Then I raised her shirt over her head and circled her nipples with my fingertips. Sliding up her body and kissing every inch along the way, I stopped to give special attention to her breasts. Her heartbeat was heavy. Continuing to kiss my way up to her neck, my dick hovered over her clit. She slightly raised her hips to show me how much she wanted it. I dipped the head down just enough to see how wet she was. Her short, quick breaths tickled my ear and her body began to slow wind beneath me.

"Tell me you want my dick." The look in her eyes was that of surrender. "Tell me you want me to fuck you."

She folded her bottom lip into her mouth and slowly released it. "I want your beautiful cock baby, I want you to fuck me," she whispered.

Like music to my ears, my dick had no choice. I dove inside her creamy wet pussy and almost lost my mind. She was so warm, wet and tight, better than any hand job I'd ever given myself. Every time I entered her, I didn't want to come out. But then again I did want to come out, just so I could go in again. When I pulled out she'd arch her back, and when I'd enter her she'd thrust her hips toward me, allowing me to fill her with all nine inches of this big dick. I fucked her slow and deep for at least half an hour. She came twice. The second time her pussy was so wet I went bananas. I fucked her like a jack hammer and bust inside her. Then with all of my weight I forced my dick as far as it would go and held her there

until I was completely empty. She let me spend the night

that night, but then she didn't call me for a week. From

the first time I saw her, I felt something different, and

every encounter after that made me want her more.

Today we've been married for three years and I wouldn't

change a thing about how we met.

What Happens in ~~Vegas~~ Sweden...?

Liquor splashed my dress as shot glasses flew by me. No regard for silk, I thought, as the bartender continued to count them down... Sweden, a place some people think is cold and boring, but not the night life where all the young and sexy gather.

"Nine!" The bartender yelled as he slid another glass by me and into the hands of an alluringly attractive man.

He had a mild innocence behind his sexy. His eyes were round and he had full, juicy lips like Kerry Washington. He caught the glass but half the liquor spilled over the back of his hand. At that moment I realized my people-watching tendencies might have gone overboard.

"Would you like one?" He asked.

"Oh, no, I don't drink. But thank you."

"Beautiful girl all dressed up, sitting at the bar but doesn't drink. Why is that?" He asked.

I swallowed hard while trying not to blush, but even more so trying not to stare at his lips.

"I'm actually here with my boyfriend, Bryan, he's in the restroom."

I paused.

"He drinks but I-I don't."

He shook his head.

"So you've *never* had a drink?"

"I have but I don't like the way alcohol tastes so I just don't… drink."

Unsure as to why this stranger made me nervous, I looked away and began to rub my arms. The warmth of a hand palmed my back and I jumped. It was Bryan. He raised his index finger to the bar tender for longer than a minute, but got no response.

"Well, we'll just sit here until they acknowledge me, how about that," he said.

Lights flashed as webs of smoke slowly motioned across the dance floor. I turned my seat to face Bryan but couldn't help but to look back one more time. There was a woman leaning over the shoulder of the handsome stranger. But that didn't stop him from making dead-on eye contact with me, and I couldn't pull myself to look away- another splash.

"Thanks, man," Bryan said.

When I looked up at him, he took the shot in one gulp.

"You're welcome," said the stranger. He stared back at me without as much as a blink, and with shoulders drawn back like a tiger preparing to eat an elephant, he and his companion approached us.

"I'm Ibrahim."

He reached for Bryan's hand.

"And this is Yasmin," he said.

Bryan shook his hand.

"Hey, thanks again for the drink, man, I'm Bryan and this is my girlfriend Alexis."

"But everyone calls me Lexi, or Lex," I said.

"*Like* sexy or sex?" Ibrahim said.

"Kind of." I forced myself to look away from his leering eyes.

The four of us sat at the bar and chatted for over an hour. Bryan and Ibrahim had many things in common. They both worked in technology, loved soccer and collected rare coins from all over the world. Yasmin and I, on the other hand, had nothing in common. She was an aspiring model from the Ukraine and I worked in accounting for a university back home in Georgia.

"We should all go back to my apartment. I have better drinks, and they're free." Ibrahim said.

"Hell yes!" Bryan said before I could object.

"It's almost two in the morning. I think we should probably go back to the resort," I said, with hopes of changing Bryan's mind.

"Come on, Lexi, let's have some fun, be-adventurous."

"Yeah, let's be adventurous, Lex," Ibrahim said.

His eyes were like slits, barely open, burning holes through me like he could read my thoughts. Surely if he could he'd know they were no good.

"It'll be fun," Yasmin said, locking her arm through mine.

"Come on- come on- come on." She chanted.

"Okay, but just for a little while."

I didn't know what to expect when we got there but Yasmin pulled meat out of the fridge and began to season it. Ibrahim had an amazing flat. He lived on top of an art studio with a pool outside his bedroom window. There were brick walls and pipes throughout the place and the ceiling had to be at least forty feet or higher.

"You guys normally grill this time of night?" I asked.

"It's a special occasion," Ibrahim said.

This time his eyes were on Bryan. I caught glimpses of him and Bryan making eye contact as if having a conversation only they understood. At first it didn't bother me, but then I became envious of it. His eyes were mine first.

Blares of ethic drums filled the room as Yasmin turned from the stereo and danced alone with her eyes closed. I sank into the couch and watched Ibrahim and Bryan take turns flipping meat on the grill. The sliding glass door to the roof was partly open and the wind blew in rhythm of the music bouncing off Yasmin's nipples. She spun around with strands of hair caught in her partly opened mouth. And then she slowed, and lowered herself to her knees. The faster the beat, the slower she moved.

"I gave Bryan all of my secrets. Now he can grill for you." Ibrahim said.

I was so enamored by Yasmin that I didn't hear them come in.

"Huh? Oh, thank you."

Yasmin rose from the floor and walked to the other side of the room, continuing her seductive dance.

"Would you like to dance?" Ibrahim asked.

"No thanks, I-"

"I'm sorry, I was talking to Bryan."

"Sure," Bryan said.

My jaw dropped immediately, I didn't know what to think. I sat there and watched Ibrahim show Bryan how to move his hips in different ways. It wasn't sexual, but definitely uncomfortably close. Yasmin slid her back up and down the wall while gyrating as if she had a partner. I considered being her partner just to make Bryan jealous.

"I think need a drink!" I said.

"You need a what?" Bryan asked.

Anything to stop this freak show, I thought.

"You heard me right. I think I need a drink."

"I'll take care of that," Ibrahim said.

Bryan sat next to me on the couch. I waited for him to acknowledge his recent actions but he just looked around the room with a wide-eyed innocence. I remember thinking to myself, *what the hell.*

"One for you, and one for you my friend," Ibrahim said as he handed each of us a glass.

Mine was red and the first sip tasted like an exotic punch. But I didn't taste any alcohol which was strange. I could always tell when someone put alcohol in anything I drank.

"I thought you didn't drink Lex." Ibrahim said. He leaned over the couch only inches away from my face.

"Well, I figured if we're going to stay here and hang out I may as well try to relax."

"Are you nervous about something?" He asked.

"No, I just figured with everyone dancing and me sitting here on the couch, I may as well just relax and relax, you know." I was still nervous.

"Yeah, I know what you mean. I'm going to check the grill and then when I come back we can all relax."

He smiled, winked and walked away.

"Sure," I said.

"Now *this* is a good drink," Bryan said.

"What is it?"

"Some kind of vodka with lemon, or maybe lime, I don't know but it's good."

Bryan and I sat knee to knee sipping our drinks but eventually found ourselves watching Yasmin, the tall and slender brunette. Every time she moved, her transparent top would graze her full, dangling breasts.

"All done," Ibrahim said.

He closed the glass door behind him and sat the food on the kitchen counter, and then joined Yasmin in her dance. With arms raised and hips swaying, she leaned her body into his, guiding his back to the wall. Ibrahim held his hands up in surrender as Yasmin grinded him. Her sheer skirt left nothing to the imagination as her body slowly wound against his. I lifted my glass, took one final gulp, and sat it on the floor next to the couch. The entire time they danced Ibrahim's eyes never left mine. He lowered his hands to Yasmin's hips and pulled her in closer to him, grinding her back. Her arm gently rose as she reached for his mouth putting two of her fingers inside and pulling his face downward to kiss her, but still, he stared at me.

My head collapsed on the couch and with sudden shoves of movement Bryan pulled himself on top of me and lifted my dress over my head. His tender kisses to my chest felt like moist tingles. My fingers fumbled over one another to unbuckle his belt, and then to unbutton and unzip his pants. While propping himself over me with his arms, I reached inside and squeezed the soft skin on his stiff cock, pulling it toward me as he hurriedly slid his pants down. My legs spread like bird wings as he stuffed himself inside me.

"Ahh-ahh."

Bryan looked me in the eyes with frowned brows and pounded me as if I were being punished for something he just realized I'd done. Then he grabbed my arms and flipped me over but he held me there. My body squirmed and throbbed for him to enter me but when he didn't I reached back and spread my cheeks open for him, tilting my pussy upward. He let my arms go and tickled between my legs with his tongue. The slight brushes up and down and then inside caused my entire body to tremble. When he finally entered me from behind it felt like my insides had been filled with thickness. I could still see his face when I closed my eyes. Picturing him looking at me made me wetter and his thrusts accommodated the moisture. My head swung from side to side as the throbbing between my legs intensified, and from across the room I looked into Bryans eyes. How could I see his face if not from behind me? I thought.

And then I knew, but I couldn't stop myself. Every second he was inside me I felt like I was about to explode. Bryan watched Ibrahim fuck me from across the room as Yasmin sucked his dick. He cupped the back of her head with both hands and shoved her face down on his lap every time Ibrahim jammed himself inside me. I came harder and louder than I ever had with Bryan. The scream was that of someone being attacked, a scream blended with a weak cry. I lay there completely empty with Ibrahim lying on my back. He closed my legs tight, and then he closed his and continued gently humping me until I came again. My body shook and throbbed so heavily that I almost curled up into the fetal position. He rolled me over and used his knees to open my legs, and with one stiff dip, he continued to fuck me. Quick short breaths, moans and half screams fled my lips. My breasts bounced off his chest causing my nipples to tingle. I could no longer make eye contact with Bryan. This time when I came, Ibrahim put his bottom lip in my mouth and I sucked it. With my knees aimed at the ceiling and his body buried between my legs, he thrust and pushed every inch of himself inside me.

"Gahhhh!" I was ashamed that I couldn't control it.

My chest rose high and sank low as I caught my breath. I rested my head on the couch and lifted my eyes to see Bryan's face. I froze. I wondered what he was thinking.

"This was fun," Yasmin said, rising from her knees. She walked into the kitchen, broke off a piece of meat, and began to nibble.

Bryan's mouth spread into a delighted half smile.

"Yeah, it was," he said.

He released a breath, zipped his pants and walked toward me.

"Damn you're sexy, Lex," he said.

Ibrahim gently rose while pulling himself out of me slowly. He slid my panties back on and kissed my thighs.

"Here you go baby," Bryan said. He stood in front of me and held my dress over my head. I sat there adjusting myself, slightly lightheaded and confused. My eyes roamed the entire floor in an effort not to connect with anyone else's. Dishes clanked as Yasmin's feet scampered across my path.

"It's time to eat you guys, come," she said.

Bryan grabbed my arm and pulled me from the couch. When we sat at the table, Ibrahim lifted his arms from his sides, reaching for Bryan and Yasmin's hands. He lowered his head and remained silent for a few seconds.

"Amen," he said.

I stared at the plate of grilled meat and salad before me, and with my head still down I gradually lifted my eyes. From across the table, chewing his food in a slow circular motion, as if he were eating me, Ibrahim's

eyes burned through my soul...still.

WTF

I woke up feeling like I had been tossed against the wall. My head was spinning, my throat was sore and all I could remember were faint chants of 'suck it- suck it' and glass eyes flying high above me. I blinked several times trying to clear my vision but it was so dark that I could barely see my hands wavering around in front of me. Staggering to my feet, the pressure between my legs became evident as I tried to stand tall, and then I knew. I had been violated. My breaths became rapid and my heart got heavy. 'Where am I?' Upon cracking the door, a ray of light from a television glared into the room. I looked back and there lay three men that I had never seen before. Quickly, I ran into the bathroom and locked the door. Looking in the mirror was almost shocking. My weave was hanging on by one track, my makeup had smeared like that of a worn out clown, and my vagina was as swollen beyond recognition. I washed my face and brushed my hair down as best as I could with my hands.

BOOM!

The bedroom door slammed, causing me to cringe.

Knock- knock- knock, "open up, I've got to piss," he said.

I cowered in the corner of the bathroom clutching my chest. "Come on, open up, I'm about to burst out here."

I had nowhere to go! There were no windows in there, and I thought my best chance of getting out would be to fight off one instead of three. I crept to the door and twisted the lock. In burst one of the men.

"Ahhhhhhhh, thank you," he said, leaning halfway over the toilet. He looked in the mirror and picked his teeth, and to my surprise he smacked my ass. "Damn girl, you put in work last night."

"What are you talking about? And who are you?"

He laughed and shook piss from the tip of his dick. "Girl, stop playing."

"Please don't hurt me." I backed into the wall.

"Are you serious?" He scrunched his face as if surprised.

"Yes, who are you?" I covered my breasts with both hands.

"Jazmine, it's me, Anthony."

"Anthony, you've got to let me out of here.

"Baby, what's going on with you?"

"Look, I don't know who you are, and I don't know who those other guys are. I just want to go home."

"Jazz, you are home. Come here." He approached me, but I sank further into the corner.

"If you touch me I will scream."

"Okay, just calm down."

Tears streamed down my face as he passed me a towel to cover myself. "What did you do to me?"

"Nothing, I just… I don't understand what's going on with you right now." He sat on top of the toilet and stared at me with sad eyes. "Can I get you anything?"

"No, I just want to leave."

"Where do you want to go?" He asked, passing me a wad of tissue.

"Home."

"This is your home, baby. Please don't cry."

Tap-tap. "Hey open up man, we have to piss out here." My bottom lip trembled at the sound of the voice through the door.

"I know you guys aren't at it again. Are you? If so, I'm next Jazmine, you promised you'd stop making me last. Now let me in before I piss myself.

My eyes lowered to the floor, rapidly moving from left to right. "What is he talking about? What did you all do to me?"

Listen, I'm going to open the door very slowly. We will explain everything, and I promise no one is going to hurt you, okay."

I drew the towel tight to my body and braced myself.

"Damn, I thought you'd never open the door." He stood in front of the toilet, and his big dick dropped low as piss ran from the tip in a thick stream. He used no hands.

"I told you Jazmine, I've been practicing this shit for three weeks." He smiled and looked at Anthony. "I told you guys, my dick was heavy." When he was done he looked at me with scrunched brows. "What's wrong, baby?"

Anthony grabbed his arm as he approached me. "Jason, wait. I think you were a little rough last night."

"ME? Why does it have to be me?" he stepped back and snatched his arm away.

"You *were* rough, and I think something happened when she hit her head because she doesn't know who we are."

"What?" Jason looked at me with watery eyes. "Baby I'm so sorry," he said, lunging toward me.

"Don't touch me!"

"Don't man, just give her some space. Jazmine you stay here for a minute. We'll be right back."

They left me, but I could hear all three of their voices through the wall. Unable to make out what they were saying, I cracked the door open to see how far I'd have to go to get out of there.

"Sweetheart." The third one appeared in front of the door, placing his knee between the door and the frame so I couldn't close it. "Are you okay?"

I backed away as he walked inside.

"Jazmine, this is Corey," said Anthony. "Come with us." He reached for my hand and gently pulled me out of the bathroom and into the living room. "Have a seat," he said. We all sat at a wood and glass dining room table next to a tall, fake plant and a pair of stilettos with a broken heel. Each of them stared at me with perplexed expressions.

"Jazmine," Anthony began, "last night, we made love. And it was amazing, as always, but this was the first time you let us all do it at once. Unfortunately some of us got carried away," he glared at Jason with hardened jaws. "You live here- with us. That's your room over there, those are your shoes and we're your men."

Could this be some kind of sick game? Each of them were so different. Anthony was dark, built like a statue and from what I saw, carrying a sledge hammer between his legs. He was Tyrese and Tyson Beckford morphed into one. And Jason was light skinned with curly hair. He had a flabby gut but not too big, he was just average, although he did have sexy eyes. And then there was Corey, he had dreads and was slightly taller than Anthony and Jason, but his European accent threw me off. As I looked at each of them, studying their faces, searching for memory of them, my eyes landed on a photo of the four of us walking on the beach. I jumped up from the table and ran into the bedroom Anthony claimed to be mine and scanned it from corner to corner. I tried on the shoes and clothes, smelled the perfume, and compared the lipstick on the dresser with what was left smeared across my face, and everything fit.

I slowly turned to the door and all three of them stood there stark naked, and shameless. Wearing one stiletto, I limped to the door. They were such gentle giants within their humble demeanors. Jason took my hand, Anthony palmed my face, and Corey hugged me from behind.

"I love you," rang in my ears in unison. As strange as the moment was, I could feel Corey's dick rise between my ass cheeks. Anthony's remained in a balance between soft and hard, and Jason's stood straight up, poking me in the thigh. Swollen pussy, sore throat and all, I couldn't stop the moisture from forming between my legs. I placed my hands on Anthony's waist and he took one stepped closer, hovering over me. His dick fell right between my legs, apparently touching Corey's, hence the quick step back he took. The silent rise and fall of Anthony's chest spoke to me in a low faint voice. His lips opened but no words came out. Corey pulled Jason by the arm and shut the door behind them as they left.

Clearly Anthony was my number one. He picked me up, wrapping my legs around his waist as he carried me to the bed. From the moment he touched my face, our eyes remained locked. Even as he dove between my legs to lick my wetness, he kept his eyes on mine. His tongue softly caressed my plump lips causing me to secrete in his mouth. The way he touched me proved our connection. The look in his eyes as he crawled up my body begged me to remember him. He laid next to me and held me tight in his arms whispering '*I love you*'. My first thought was to just lie there and let him hold me, let time pass to see how things would unfold, but my body responded to him as if it knew him better than I could ever remember. I pulled his arms, motioning for him to lie on top of me, and he complied. His penis guided itself inside me with ease. I remained at the peak of an orgasm from the moment of his entry. My pussy was so sore that he fucked me un-sore, until I could only feel the wetness pouring out of me like a water hose. His grunts forced everything in me out at once, and I could feel his stiff dick throbbing, pouring his love juices into my juicy peach. Gently he pulled his dick out and stood next to the bed. I reached for him to come back, I was still horny.

"Just a second, baby," he said. My body heaved up and down on the bed, waiting and ready for him to enter me again. Instead he opened the door and Jason approached the bed.

"May I enter you, baby?" he asked, eyes lowered to the floor as if awaiting permission to touch me.

"Yes."

Immediately, he locked eyes with me and climbed on the bed. The sight of his dick frightened me, it was so big. But one inch at a time, he lowered himself inside me.

"Oh!" I screamed.

It was amazing. What I felt for one, I felt for the other, and not just sexual. The emotions I felt for them were unexplainable. My body knew them, and loved them, and needed them. The entire time he was inside me was like a wild ride. My eyes remained wide and each time he entered me I could feel juices exiting to give him all the room he needed. His dick hit the back wall of my pussy and he held it there without movement until I came… Then he turned me over and entered from behind while fingering my clit. It only took a matter of seconds before I released a scream that could have caused the neighbors to call the cops. My walls flooded with moisture and everything waist down trembled. As I lay face down on the bed, he kissed my earlobe and whispered, "I'm usually last." I remained lying there, pussy still contracting.

"More," I moaned in a wounded tone.

The slight brush of cold fingertips caressed my thighs. I looked back and into the eyes of Corey. He moved his dreads to the side and kissed me while spreading my ass cheeks. He climbed on top of me and rode me like a horse. I grabbed the sheets, stuffing them in my mouth to smother the exaggerated moans I had no control of. As if I weighed nothing, he flipped me over and gutted me out. It felt so good I couldn't close my mouth. All I could do was grab the sheets and squirm away from him.

"Where you think your ass going, huh?" He lifted my legs above my head and spanked his body against mine splashing our combined juices while holding my thighs. Smack-smack-smack-smack and there it was… the chanting of suck-it, the smacking sound, and their eyes connecting with mine. Like a lion's roar, his orgasm caused the air to rumble. He squeezed me down on his five inch, fat, thick dick and tickled the entire circumference of my pussy until I came. Sweat raced down my chest as he remained on his knees looking down at me. Slowly, I sat up only to see that Anthony and

Jason sitting on the chase watching us. Corey moved to the foot of the bed. I tucked the sheets between my legs and looked at each of them. The anticipation in their eyes told me they wanted an answer. Do you remember us? Aside from the chants and their eyes from the night before, I didn't, but deep inside I knew they were mine.

Whose is it?

I love sex more than most men, I'm sure of it. When you're thinking about what to wear, what you're going to eat or how much money you have, I'm thinking about dick. Not just any dick though, Cameron's dick, with his super chocolate ass. He gives a whole new meaning doggy style, and I love it!

"Morning, baby," Cameron said as I walked into the kitchen. He sat at the table with one hand stretched above his head, and the other in his boxers while watching the news.

"Morning, sweetheart." I sat in his lap and kissed his forehead. "You want breakfast?"

"Hell yeah," he said. I stood and walked to the stove but looked back to make sure he was watching my ass.

While reaching for the overhead cabinet my t-shirt slightly rose, revealing the bottom of my cheeks, and confirming that I had on no panties. Peering over my shoulder, I could see Cameron's half smile and low cut eyes.

"Come here," he said.

I often played coy just to get a rise out of him, a stiff, thick rise as a matter of fact. He shifted in his seat but I ignored his request and continued banging pots. No sooner than I turned around to tease him once again, there Cameron was, standing right behind me.

"Didn't I tell you to come here?" He whispered, placing his hands on my hips. He took the pot from the stove and sat it on the floor in front of me. "Pick it up," he said.

With bent knees, I reached for the pot.

"Uh- uh, slowly." He placed the palm of his hand on the small of my back. Before I could reach the handle of the pot, his tongue was inside me. With nothing to balance myself, I had no choice but to hit my knees. Cameron slid beneath me and repositioned himself, sitting me on his face. He treated me like an orange, pulling and squeezing my ass while driving his tongue in and out of my soppily wet pussy. He licked and sucked my lips, and grinded his tongue between my legs until I came. My thighs shook and tightened around his face as my body jerked. I straddled him with my palms pressed to the floor as he drank my sweet juices. Pushing my thighs upward, Cameron stared into my pussy, continuing to watch cum drip from my lips to his.

"Don't move," he said.

I remained hovered over him on all fours. He got on his knees behind me and tapped his dick on my ass cheeks, occasionally caressing his shaft between my legs.

He knew how to keep me wet. My breaths shortened, and my pussy throbbed but no matter how many times I shoved my ass against his groin, he made me wait.

"Please," I begged, "please baby, give it to me." He spanked my ass with his dick again, and again.

"Whose pussy is this?" He asked.

I squirmed while reaching back for his dick but he wouldn't let me touch it. "This is Cameron's pussy," I whined.

"I can't hear you."

"This is your pussy Cameron, it's yours baby."

The pressure of his meaty dick penetrated my tiny hole until he lie snug inside me.

"Damn," he said, squeezing my hips with both hands.

"Baby, your dick feels so good."

Cameron lifted my knees from the floor and pulled me all the way down on his lap. With every deep thrust, I could feel his oversized balls grinding against my clit.

"Cameron, I love the way you fuck me."

My whispers always turned him on. He moaned and grunted, and then he stuck his thumb in my ass and fucked me harder, and faster. My arms weakened, moments away from giving out. He picked me up, his dick still inside me, and lay me face down on the kitchen table. With every in and out motion of his dick, he used the same rhythm with his thumb. It only took about nine or so pumps before I exploded cum, covering his dick and dripping down his balls. And oh, how my baby loves it wet. He slightly lifted my ass and slammed be down on his dick over and over until he released a scream filled with masculine energy.

"Shit!" He shouted. Then he held me down on his bone while pushing every inch of himself inside me. I could feel his dick swelling, wavering between hard and soft. His surrender allowed me to slide off of him, and once again I hit my knees, but this time facing him. The contractions of his dick spurting cum thrusts turned me on. I opened my mouth, filling it with his pipe, causing him to wince and grab the back of his head with both hands.

"I fucking love you, girl."

I rose from my knees, still jacking him off with one hand while circling his nipple with my tongue. Making my way up to his neck, I leaned in and asked, "Whose dick is this?"

"This dick belongs to you, baby."

Demetrius's Mouth...

I met Demetrius three months ago on a blind date. He's been hanging in there as far as my 'no sex before monogamy' rule but he sure does have a slick ass mouth. We've kissed a couple of times and he even let me get away with grinding on his dick, but I know most of the shit he talks comes from the frustration of not being able to touch me. The thing is, we can't both have it our way. He wants to be free to date other people and I get that, but I refuse to end up with a health issue or getting pregnant by a player, so until he's ready to sit his ass down, he will remain frustrated.

Sunday morning, like clock-work, he picked me up for church and to my surprise he was nice to me all day. I wondered if something was wrong, or if he'd been with someone else so I asked, but he swore to me he hadn't and that everything was fine. That evening he cooked for me for the first time, and it was actually good.

We cuddled on the couch and watched a movie, but I couldn't relax; all of a sudden he was everything I wanted, but this wasn't like him.

"What are you up to?" I abruptly asked.

"What are you talking about, I'm just watching the movie."

"Nah, you know what I mean. What's going on with you?"

"Baby I don't know what you're talking about. Come here, just lie back with me and watch the movie, okay?"

I laid back, but his dick was brick hard, running down the middle of my spine.

"I'm sorry," he said, I'll move so you don't have to deal with that tonight."

I felt bad, I'm giving him a hard time and he's being so sweet to me. He slid from beneath me and raised from the couch.

"You don't have to move."

"You sure?"

"Yeah, I'm sure."

He sat between my legs and laid his head on my stomach. Halfway through the movie he began to squirm as if he couldn't get comfortable. His head rubbed against my clit, and every time he moved, my cotton skirt raised a little bit higher.

"Baby, did you see that? That dude is funny as hell." Every word that came out of his mouth including his laughter, caused a warm vibration between my legs. He turned and positioned himself sideways, laying his face directly on my wet pussy lips.

"Mmm, baby this is like the best pillow in the world. I can just go to sleep right here."

More vibrations- now I'm throbbing, and I know he feels it.

"I need to use the restroom," I said, hoping to go dry myself and calm down.

"Um-um, you ain't going nowhere," he said, rolling onto his stomach. He took his finger and caressed the edge of my sheer, pink panties while looking at me. With his eyes locked on mine, he pulled his mouth closer to my body, and placed his warm tongue between my legs. I died inside when he licked me. All of my inhabitations, every rule I had, and any common sense I carried around like a blue print were gone. He ripped a small hole in my panties and stuck his tongue through it to eat me. The hairs from his goatee ran up and down my inner thighs as I pulled him further inside. His lips felt like a pair of juicy balls and his tongue- a small dick. Every time I looked down at his sexy caramel skin I kicked myself for making him wait. The irony… his mouth was the one thing that allowed me to hold out, and now it's the one thing that's making me want him to fuck

me.

What's your fantasy?

"Baby, what's your fantasy?"

"You. I imagine me picking you up from work on a Thursday and spending the entire day doing whatever you want. That night I check us into a five star hotel. I run you a bath and after you're all cleaned up I give you an oral massage starting with your feet. That's right, I suck your toes first and then nibble on your ankle bones, easing my way up to those juicy thighs. I can feel the heat from your pussy trying to rush me but I take my time. Continuing to make my way up your body, I skip your strawberry patch and stick my tongue in your navel. Then I drag it all the way up to your raisin like nipples. Resting my naked body on top of yours, I can feel the moisture between your legs increasing. I use my knee to open them a bit wider before sticking my tongue down your throat. At that point you can't take my thunder stick caressing your clit so you pull my ass toward you but I resist. I want to eat you first, but you grind your hips, blindly searching for my dick. The waves your body assert weaken my manhood. I surrender, slipping and sliding between your legs until my Jimmy establishes power firing off like a rocket into your love nest. Your sultry moans make me go deep- deeper- deepest. Wet ass pussy. I fuck you slow, collecting mental photographs of every sex face you own. With your mouth wide open, gasping for air, I lift your soft body from the bed and sit you on my lap. That's right, ride that dick, baby. DAMN! There's no sight more beautiful than your pussy sliding up and down on my cum-filled cock. Your breasts bounce as sweat drips down that middle space between them. Then you lay on top of me. I squeeze your hips, lifting your ass up and down to keep the momentum of bang, bang, bang. Now you kiss me, sucking my bottom lip, gliding your tongue down my neck, and gently licking my earlobe.

Tension runs through my body like feathers stroking me from the inside. I hold you tighter, and slow things down and take over the rhythm. We both wind and grind our bodies to the flow of our pausing breaths. Each time you come down on my dick, holding for just a second, your thighs tremble. The hesitations in your exhales tell me your orgasm is on its way. Clearly my mission is to please you so I allow nature to take its course as your creamy cum slides down my dick. The mild scream filled moan you release grants me permission to proceed. I hold you down on my lap while forcing thrusts of my man flow inside your sweet berry patch... Sweetheart, why are you looking at me like that?"

"Because clearly my husband wants to fuck me tonight."

"You damn right!"

Did Someone Scream the R Word?

The night was hot like that of Las Vegas weather but I knew I was still in Savannah. Standing in the doorway, starring out at the night sky, the moon starred back at me telling a sad story. I took a hefty sip of wine then closed my robe and turned to go back inside.

Startled by a rustling of the bushes, I looked down from the balcony and saw a cat pawing at the thistle. "Goodness, I must be jumpy tonight." Aimlessly tossing pebbles was the only recourse I had to rid me of my terrible fear of cats. "Scat, you old furry pussy!" I shouted, backing my way inside. I sashayed down the corridor as my robe glided open while brushing the floor. Just as I passed the dining room window, a shadowy figure moved from one side to the other. At first glance I thought someone was inside, but as I peered around the corner there was no one. I gulped from my glass of wine and strolled into the bedroom. There I stood in front of an oval shaped mirror admiring my slight nakedness hidden beneath the thin sheer fabric draped across my shoulders. I let the robe fall to the floor creating the illusion of a milky puddle around my feet. Nearly floating across the room, I turned on some music as I prepared to get dressed for my girlfriend's party.

After laying several garments across the bed, I felt a cool breeze brush by me. "What in the world," I said as I crept beyond the doorframe. Wearing only a pair of black lace panties, I made my way down the narrow hallway and paused at the sight of my front door left wide open. Hurriedly, I closed the door and turned the lock. Using my arms as covering for my breasts, I hugged the wall all the way back to my bedroom, but nothing prepared me for the sight of the clothes I left sprawled across the bed now neatly folded, one item on top of the other. I froze in the doorway and perused the entire room, afraid to enter. I thought to myself, *'who could possibly be in here, how fast I can get out of here, and what I can throw on to avoid running out of the house naked?'* Those thoughts rushed my mind within milliseconds and all of a sudden the lights went out. I screamed, wondering if whoever it was could see me right where I stood. Were they in my bedroom or had they left the house? Which way should *I* run?

I stood there for what felt like minutes, and nothing happened. I didn't hear any movement and as tipsy as I was, I began to wonder if I had folded the clothes myself, and if the power had simply gone out. I staggered to the window to see if the neighbors had also lost power, but panic set in as their lights beamed through the blinds. While slowly backing away from the window and reaching for the t-shirt on my bed, I could feel his presence behind me. There was no time scream before he gaged me. Kicking my legs back and forth trying to break away from his grip, I was helplessly pinned to the bed. He blindfolded me but left my hands free.

"If you scream, you'll regret it," he said. I remained silent as he tore my panties off and entered me. The slight pain of his dry entrance caused me to bite my bottom lip. Once inside me, he didn't move at first. He just stayed there, deep inside me, sucking my breasts and rubbing my thighs. I didn't know how to feel. At first I was afraid, and my heart was beating so fast and hard that it felt like something was hitting my entire body in rhythm.

The more he seduced me, the beat of my hart began to move from my chest to my vagina. The tremble of his body told me that he felt the throbbing wetness between my legs. He began to glide in and out of me with force. I pushed his shoulders trying to get him off of me but he pinned my hands above my head and slammed his body down on top of mine.

"Take this dick! Take it! Take it!" He chanted over, and over. I was so upset with my body for not being as angry as my mind. The deeper he stroked me, the more I began to give it back. His deep, long, quick strokes at the speed of a nutri-bullet left my mouth frozen open. I had never been so juicy. The pulsating jerks of his ejaculation caused me to rain down on his dick in excess. My reaction to this act almost frightened me. I wondered if I was as twisted as a rapist. He slowly removed my blindfold but the look in his eyes was that of confusion, as if he didn't know what to do next. I cupped his face in my hands and said "Baby, next time be a fireman."